Illustrations by Dianna Bonder

A PACIFIC ALPHABET

Text by Margriet Ruurs

WALRUS

B O O K S

Aa

A day on the beach, full of sand, sun, and fish
makes me believe I could have any wish.

Albatross, albatross, up in the air—
with wings like yours, I could fly
anywhere!

Bb

Blue whales make bubbles
as they dive and they breach
from the tip of Alaska
to a Mexican beach.

I'd love to blow bubbles just like a whale
at night in the tub with my soap
and my pail.

Cc

The captain is casting a cautious eye on the cirrus and cumulus clouds in the sky.

Dd

Despite the damp drizzle
I do enjoy roaming
down by the dock where
I do my beachcombing.

My dogs and my ducklings all dawdle along
as I gather up driftwood while humming a song.

Ee

Ebb is my favorite
tide to explore
exquisite shells on the
exposed ocean floor.

In the foggy forest among wet ferns and logs,
I search for fairies but only find frogs.
I know that they live here beneath all the flowers;
they're as big as my finger and have magical powers!

Gg

When gale winds gust across the gray sky,
seagulls and geese find it too hard to fly.

On such a grim
and blustery day,
I gather my friends
to chase clouds away.

Hh

Humongous humpback whales head north,
while a hovering helicopter tracks their course.

li

In summer I swim in the inky blue sea,
but in winter it is simply too icy for me.
My fingers are freezing and so are my toes,
while icicles hang
off the tip of my nose!

Jellyfish, jellyfish,
how do you do?
I wish I could find
peanut butter fish,
too!

Jj

Kk

Look at this marvelous kelp that I've found,
it's perfect for jumping and twirling around!

But when I'm at the beach
my favorite thing
is flying a kite
way up on a string.

Leaking ships sometimes get lost at sea,
everyone wonders where they could be.
The lighthouse keeper, in his yellow raincoat,
locates the crew with his little lifeboat.

Ll

Mm

Mystical mermaids in misty moonlight
at midnight are a magnificent sight!
Monarchs and moths float to the moon
while marlins move to
a magical tune.

Nn

The S.S. *Neptune*, piled neatly with freight,
navigates north up the long narrow strait.

Over the railing, I look at the ocean
where oodles of octopus cause a commotion!
And oh, those outrageous orcas and otters
splishing and splashing around in the waters.

Peering at the Pacific, what do I see?
Pirates approaching pelican and me!

Pods of playful porpoises plunging down deep—
Where do they go to?
Where do they sleep?

P p

Quaint cottages stand,
and giant trees reach
down the calm, quiet coast
at Qualicum Beach.

Red raspberries grow
    at the rain forest's shore
  where I reap razor clams,
    rocks and much more.

Ss

See the starfish and scallops stuck in the sand?
I carefully scoop them up
into my hand.
The sound in my seashell
is of waves and a breeze,
a swordfish's secrets and
a sea horse's sneeze!

Tt

Ten thousand tentacles
tickle my toe
where turquoise
anemones and
turretshells grow.

Uu

Urchins are utterly
amazing to me:
spiky umbrellas
under the sea.

Vv

Captain Vancouver's vessel sailed forth.
He crossed the Pacific,
then ventured up north,

where he found a spot he thought was terrific—
it's now called Vancouver, to be more specific.

Ww

When the winds start to whip
and the weather gets rough,
I like to watch whitecaps
way up on a bluff,
where water won't splash me
when the waves get too high,
and walruses wait
for the whales to go by.

Xx

I sit on the boardwalk above the warm sand
and listen to the music of the xylophone band.

While taking a trip
on a yacht yesterday
I dreamed of sailing
to China,
so far, far away.

Zz

Our trusty Zodiac can zoom mighty quick;
zigzagging on waves is our own special trick.
Zipping across the ocean is really terrific,
from Anchorage to Zenith—anywhere on the Pacific!

Did you find the hidden letter on each page?
What other things can you find?

Aa abalone, albacore, albatross, algae, amethyst, anchor, antennae, ants, apples, apricot, ark, arm, arrow, artichoke, asters, auklets

Bb ball, bar of soap, bath towel, bathtub, bear head, bedroom slippers, belt, blue whale, boat, brush, bubbles, bucket

Cc can, candle, cane, cap, captain, carrots, cat, cirrus clouds, clams, clock, coat, cone shells, cord, cork, corn on the cob, crab, crest, crow, crow's nest, cumulus clouds, cup

Dd Dalmation, dock, dogs, dragonflies, driftwood, drizzle, drum, ducks,

Ee eagles, ear, earwig, eggs, elbow patch, elephant seals, envelope, eye

Ff fairies, feather, ferns, fingers, flowers, forest, frogs, fungus

Gg geese, giant clams, glass, gold chains, goldfish, grapefruit, grapes, grass, grasshopper, grouse, guitar, gulls

Hh halibut, helicopter, heron, honeybees, humpback whales

Ii ice, iceberg, ice cream cone, ice fishing, iguana, inflatable dinghy, ink well, iris, iron, ivy

Jj jack in the box, jackrabbit, jacksmelt, jade necklace, jars, jay, jelly, jellyfish, jewellery, jug, jumper

Kk kayak, kelp, keys, king, kites, kitten, knapsack

Ll lantern, lemons, lens (telescope), lifeboat, lifeguard, lightbulb, lighthouse, limes, line (fishing), ling cod, lock, lures

Mm mackerel, magnolias, man on the moon, marlin, matchstick, mermaids, mice, mirror, moon, moonlight, moon shell, moths, mouth

Nn nails, nautilus shell, necklace, needle, *Neptune*, nest, nets, newspaper, newt, nimbostratus clouds, nose, note, nutcracker, nuts, nutshell

Oo oar, ocean, octopus, oranges, orcas, otters, oyster

Pp pail, pear, pearl, pelican, periscope, pig, pigeon, pirate flag, pizza, plaice, plankton, plug, porcupine, porpoises, pot, potatoes, puffins

Qq quail, quiet, quill, quilt

Rr rabbit, raccoon, rainbow, rain forest, raspberries, raven, razor clams, rocks

Ss sailboat, salmon, sand dollar, saxophone, scales, scallop, sea, sea horse, seashore, shells, skate, smelt, snail, snare drum, sole, suspenders

Tt tentacles, toad, toes, tulips, tuna, turretshells

Uu ukulele, umbrella, underwear, unicycle, urchins

Vv Captain Vancouver, vessel, vine, violin, volleyball, vulture

Ww walking stick, walruses, watch, water, waves, weather vane, west, whales, wheel, wheelbarrow, whiskers, whistle, whitecaps, wood, woodpecker, wool coat, worm

Xx X-ray, xylophone

Yy yacht, yams, yardstick, yarn, yellow jackets, yellowthroat bird, yolk, yo-yo, yucca plant

Zz zebra, zipper, Zodiac®, zucchini

Text copyright © 2001 by Margriet Ruurs
Illustrations copyright © 2001 by Dianna Bonder
Walrus Books
First paperback edition 2003
Fourth paperback printing 2009

Thank you to Zodiac Hurricane Technologies Inc. for allowing us to use the registered trade name Zodiac® in this book.

Edited by Michelle R. McCann
Proofread by Kathy Evans
Photography by Weekes Photo Graphics
Cover and interior design by Tanya Lloyd/Spotlight Designs
Printed and bound in China

LIBRARY AND ARCHIVES CANADA CATALOGUING IN PUBLICATION
Ruurs, Margriet, 1952–
    A Pacific alphabet / text by Margriet Ruurs; illustrations by Dianna Bonder, illustrator.

    ISBN 10 1-55285-264-4 (bound).—ISBN 10 1-55285-521-X (pbk.).
    ISBN 13 978-1-55285-521-8 (pbk.)

    1. English language—Alphabet—Juvenile literature.
2. Pacific Coast (B.C.)—Pictorial works—Juvenile literature.
I. Bonder, Dianna, 1970– II. Title.
PE1155.R883 2001   j421'.1   C2001-910974-1

The publisher acknowledges the financial support of the Canada Council for the Arts, the British Columbia Arts Council, and the Government of Canada through the Book Publishing Industry Development Program (BPIDP). Whitecap Books also acknowledges the financial support of the Province of British Columbia through the Book Publishing Tax Credit.

BRITISH COLUMBIA ARTS COUNCIL   Canada Council for the Arts Conseil des Arts du Canada